At Arm's Length

Shirley Jordan

authorHOUSE®

AuthorHouse™
1663 Liberty Drive
Bloomington, IN 47403
www.authorhouse.com
Phone: 1 (800) 839-8640

Published by AuthorHouse 07/22/2015

ISBN: 978-1-5049-2215-9 (sc)
ISBN: 978-1-5049-2216-6 (e)

Chapter 1

Friendship

We were friends forever. We shared secrets that would break another person's heart and probably put some people away for life. I thought I knew everything about her, because she knew everything about me. I held back nothing. If there was anyone that I knew I could trust my life's secrets with, it would have been my best friend Michelle. I just didn't know the secrets we kept for each other would end up destroying our friendship.

From the day we met in the first grade, we became best friends. You could almost count the times when people didn't see us together. People actually thought we were sisters, because when you saw me, you would see her. If I wasn't at her house, she would be at mine. We even shared each other's families. Her family was mine and my family was hers. We felt at home, no matter whose house we were in.

We shared each other's clothes, shoes and we even shared the same boyfriend once. Nothing was too good or too hard for us to concur as long as we were together. I thought we would be friends forever.

We sometimes dressed alike and told people we were cousins instead of best friends. Michelle looked a little older than me, but I was the oldest by three months. People used to ask if we were twins and we would say no, but I don't remember anyone asking who was the oldest.

We said we would move in with each other when we got older. We even wanted to work at the same place of business and save our money to purchase nice furniture. Our plans were to split all the bills in half, so we could have lots of money left over to buy pretty clothes and travel together, but I guess nothing last forever. It was only wishful thinking on my part.

As we got older, my so called best friend that I thought would be my friend for life, turned against me. Things were great in elementary school, when we shared the same boyfriend, but now we were in junior high and Michelle began to take more interest in boys much sooner than I did. She no longer wanted to do the things we made plans to do for the future.

We always did things together, but when she met and fell in love with a football player name Kenneth, in junior high school. She forgot all about me, and there was no way in hell she was going to share this boyfriend with me. She no longer wanted to do any of the things that we used to do.

I understood the whole boyfriend thing, but what about our friendship?

Did it have to end just because she met a guy?

It was as if she had a new best friend and they did all the things we used to do together. Michelle even told him all of my secrets. By the time the news got back to me. Words were added and twisted to make me look bad.

Other classmates were looking at me differently and some would even turn their noses up at me, as if I had done something wrong. I had never felt so along before.

I tried calling Michelle to ask her if she said the things that were coming back to me, or was it her boyfriend saying all the twisted bad things about me, just to keep us apart. My calls were unanswered.

This guy had really taken over my best friend's mind. She wanted nothing to do with me. I did nothing or said nothing to make her turn her back on me, and not want to be my best friend anymore.

Michelle had totally changed. She would pass by me in the hallways at school, and turn her head the other way, so she wouldn't have to speak to me. I wasn't sure if she was ignoring me, because of all the lies that were going on around the school, or if she was too ashamed to look at me, because of the friendship we used to have and what it had become. It was a great friendship gone bad for no reason.

I just couldn't forget about her. She knew everything about me, so how could she let someone from out of nowhere come between us and end our lifelong friendship. We had known each other since first grade and there was a lot of history between us. She had found herself another group of friends that were affiliated with her boyfriend. Now her friends were cheerleaders and football players.

So I decided to give her and her boyfriend all the time they needed together, by keeping both of them at arm's length.

I loved her like a sister. I knew the friends that she was hanging around, would soon turn their backs on her like she turned on me. So I decided to put everything to pass and wait for her to come to me for help.

I knew that the time would come for her to need me, because she depended on me for everything when we were best friends. The friends she was hanging with didn't have to work hard in school to earn their grades, because they were athletes and cheerleaders. During our school years, anyone that did any type of sports for the school had a special kind of leeway with their grades, because the school had their backs, like I had Michelle's back since first grade.

Michelle was only a girlfriend of a football player and she wasn't able to keep up with her book work, and hang with her new friends, because she used to rely on me, when it came to school work.

There were other girls in the group that was only girlfriends of football players, but I didn't know if they served the same purpose as Michelle.

Michelle's boyfriend, Kenneth thought Michelle could do his school work for him, while he played the field with other girls. What he didn't know, was Michelle's school work was done by me. I just let her take the credit, so people would think she was as smart.

When we were together, I helped Michelle with her school work and let her take all the credit, so she would feel good about herself. Now she was on her own, her grades were falling fast.

What Michelle didn't know, was the fact of Kenneth trying to talk to me first. When I turned him down, he went to Michelle, hoping she wouldn't turn him down, and she didn't.

I never told Michelle about Kenneth's secret. I guess that's why he told her a lot of negative things about me. He made sure I kept his secret, because Michelle didn't want anything to do with me.

Kenneth thought Michelle was very smart. He chose her to be his girlfriend, so she could do all of his homework, while he practiced football. He had another girlfriend that Michelle didn't know about. She was doing most of his class work. But when I tried to tell Michelle, she didn't want to listen.

She said that I was jealous of her, because she had a boyfriend that was a football player, and he was very popular in school. I tried telling her that being popular in school doesn't get you ahead when you are making bad grades.

I wanted to tell her that Kenneth asked me to be his girlfriend first, but I knew it would only put more wood on the flame, and the fire was already flaming hot. So I let Michelle continue to be used by the famous football player. But she was right about one thing, I was jealous, but not because of the reason, she thought I was jealous for. I was jealous because Kenneth ruined our friendship and turned my best friend against me.

Kenneth's grades began to drop, because Michelle didn't have a clue as to what she was doing, when she was trying to do his homework. So she tried asking the cheerleaders for help. Her excuse was she was failing in her class work trying to do Kenneth's class work.

Out of the six cheerleader friends Michelle was hanging with, only one was smart enough to pass on a C average. Her name was Pam, and she was chosen to be a girlfriend, because of the same reason Michelle was chosen. Her boyfriend had her doing, not only his homework, but she was doing his class work as well, while he practiced football and chased other girls around the school with Kenneth.

When Michelle asked Pam to help her with Kenneth's homework, Pam became furious. She said that she had enough to do, by doing not only Michael's homework and class work, but she had to do her homework as well. She didn't have time to stop and show someone else how it was done.

Pam told Michael that Michelle asked her to show her how to do Kenneth's homework and Michael told Kenneth. When Kenneth found out Michelle didn't know how to do his homework, he got very upset with her. He told her that she was the reason his grades were falling, and the coach had him to practicing harder and play less during football games, than what he would usually play. Kenneth was used to starting the football games, but now the couch had him playing towards the end of each game. His grades were barely passing, but he had that leeway that kept him above water. Coach knew if it wasn't for Kenneth being on the football team, he wouldn't pass to the next grade and Kenneth blamed Michelle for his failure. He told Michelle that it was over between them. He said he wanted her to lose his telephone number and to forget that she ever knew him.

Michelle didn't know I was friends with Pam. She was keeping me up to date with all the drama that was going on with the entire football players and their girlfriends. While Michelle was hanging with her, so call new friends. I continued to hang with our old friends and some of her cheerleaders friends.

I knew more of what was going on with Michelle, than she knew about me, because Kenneth kept her away from me. I was what you would call a true friend and friendship meant a lot to me. I would never turn my back on someone, just because I met someone new or even if I found myself a fairly good boyfriend. I was the type of person that cared about everyone's feeling. I tried to make sure that everyone fitted in with me, no matter how smart they were.

I never used my education against any of my friends, I just thought I caught on to things a little faster than they did, because I refused to be ghetto and uneducated. I always thought learning was the key, and it would unlock the doors for better things for me. It was up to others to choose their pathway of learning.

I didn't agree with the way Kenneth and Michael's pathway of learning, because I thought they were cheating their selves out of a good education. But if that's what they wanted out of life, who was I to change their minds?

I thought they would learn about their mistakes of life as they lived life. After all, life is the best experience. You can't learn right from wrong if you've never done any wrong to learn from.

After Kenneth kicked Michelle to the curb, she tried to come back to the friends she turned her back on, to become a football player's girlfriend, and become popular. But no one would accept her back. They told her that she was wrong for the way she treated me. They said that I was always there for her and I would never spread rumors about her, like she did to me.

When the story got back to me, that Michelle was trying to come back to the other side of the friendship line, I told everyone to let her back in. I told them to just keep her at arm's length, just in case she decides to turn her back on them again. For some reason I was highly respected by all of my friends, and Michelle didn't like that. She became jealous of me. Instead of wanting to be like me, she wanted to become me, but it was a challenge for her. No one trusted her after what she tried to do to me. So she decided, if she couldn't be like me, then she would destroy my credibility.

There were some things that I told Michelle when we were much younger and she decided to spread my bad news with everyone we knew. When the news got to Pam, she immediately called me to let me know what Michelle was trying to do to me. Pam was so upset with Michelle. She called her and told her that she was wrong for what she was trying to do. She said that I was a good friend to everyone and I was the one, who told the other friends to give Michelle another chance, after she had turned her back on everyone.

Pam told Michelle that having a boyfriend that's a football player wasn't all that. She said there were pros and cons to the madness of being there girlfriend. They were only football player girlfriends and nothing more. They let themselves be used, just to become popular and that was disrespectful to any girl. She also told Michelle that she learned that from me, and it made a lot of sense to her, because she was also being used by Michael. If she didn't have time to do his homework, he would get upset with her. When she tried to explain to him that she had to do her homework too. Michael didn't want to hear it. He would say Pam was making excuses, so she wouldn't have to do his work.

Meanwhile, Michelle found out she was pregnant with Kenneth's baby. She was trying to figure out how she should tell him. She thought he would be happy to become a father, so she called him and asked if she could come over to his house, so they could talk.

Kenneth thought Michelle wanted to have sex with him, so he agreed to see her. When she told him the news about the baby, he said that the baby wasn't his. He told her that he knew she was sleeping with other football players and he never wanted to talk to her again.

Michelle wasn't expecting Kenneth to accuse her of sleeping with anyone else. He knew he was the first and only. She just knew he would be happy to become a father. But Kenneth had other plans for his future. He wanted to become a famous football player and a baby was nowhere in his future plans. Michelle didn't know what to do or who she could turn to. She had destroyed our friendship and she didn't want her cheerleader friends to know of the big mistake she had made getting pregnant.

Michelle had an older brother name Michael and he was a famous basketball player at TSU. She told him, she was pregnant and the baby daddy didn't want to have anything to do with her nor the baby. Michael wanted Michelle to take him to Kenneth's house so he could talk to him, but Michelle refused. She knew Michael was upset and she didn't want him to do anything to make Kenneth anymore upset with her, than he already was.

Michael took Michelle to an abortion clinic. He didn't want her to mess up her life, trying to raise a baby alone. Since Michelle wasn't old enough to sign the abortion papers, Michael signed the papers as her guardian.

Michelle and Michael never told their mother about Michelle's secret. They didn't know how their mother would accept the news. Michelle was the baby of the family and only sixteen years old, about to become a single mother. She wasn't sure if her mother could handle that.

Her secret was kept between the both of them, but other people outside of the family knew about it, and Michelle was afraid of someone telling her secret to her parents.

When the news got back to me, I tried calling Michelle, to see if she needed a shoulder to lean on. Having an abortion was a serious thing and I knew she needed a friend to talk to. I still wanted Michelle as a friend, but after being betrayed by my best friend, I just wanted to be there for her at her time of need. If she wanted to talk to me about what she was going through, I was there to listen. And if she wanted my advice on anything, I was there to give it to her. But I refused to do anything more.

I'd seemed to keep all other friends at arm's length too. I didn't want to put myself in another bad situation. I only said things to people that I didn't mind getting out. So if it came back to me, it wouldn't be such a big deal.

During all this time, Michelle never apologized to me. She thought she would never need me again. But this secret was very important to her. She knew if her secret got back to her parents, that her brother signed papers for her to have an abortion without their permission, would destroy her. It would not only destroy her life, but it would destroy Michael's life as well.

Michelle thought hard and long before she finally decided to call me. She sounded so pitiful on the phone. She asked me if she could come over so we could talk. I told her sure. I told her I was waiting for her phone call.

When she did come over, she looked sick. I asked if she was okay. She asked if I knew about the abortion. I told her yes, I knew about it the same day that it happen. She asked me if she was wrong for having the abortion and I told her what I thought about the situation. I said, it was a life that she took and she would have to answer to God about it when the time comes. She told me that she was scared. She couldn't stop thinking about the baby. She said she wanted her baby, but Michael told her that she was too young to become a mother, especially when the baby daddy was refusing to claim the baby.

I asked her if she tried talking to Kenneth before having the abortion, and she told me that he didn't want to have anything to do with her, because she was the cause of him not playing football. His grades had fallen so bad. The coach had him to sit on the bench for three games.

I told her that the decision was already made and she couldn't turn back the hands of time. So just accept the mistake that she made and move on. I didn't know what it was like to have an abortion, so I couldn't tell her what she wanted to hear. I knew she should be having some difficult thoughts in her head.

Most young girls that get pregnant at a young age have abortions, because they aren't ready to become a parent and didn't want to ruin their lives. They are confused and didn't know if they could be a good parent and finish school. But Michelle really wanted to keep her baby. She thought Kenneth would want her back, if she had a son for him. But she didn't know how to face him. She wanted me to talk to him for her. She said that he would listen to me, because I was smart. I told her that smart didn't have anything to do with it, but she should have been smart enough to use protection to avoid having an aborting.

Michelle had the saddest look on her face after hearing the horrible words that came out of my mouth. So I apologized and said I would talk to Kenneth for her. But when I went to Kenneth, he said Michelle had sex with more than three of the football players and he wasn't sure if the baby was his or one of the other players. I went back to Michelle and told her what Kenneth told me and she was dumbfounded. She couldn't believe what Kenneth told me. She said that Kenneth wanted her to have sex with the other football players because they were his buddies but she refused to do it. Kenneth told her, if she loved him, she would have sex with the other football players. So I asked her if she had sex with the other player and she said no. She said, couldn't do it with Kenneth the first time he asked her to have sex with him. She said Kenneth wanted some of his football friends to watch them as they had sex and she wasn't comfortable with that.

Later, when she and Kenneth were alone, he asked her again and she didn't want to lose him, so she gave in, even though she wasn't ready. She thought she had gained his trust. He was her first and she told him that she wanted him to be her only. But when he asked her to do it with one football player at a time, she was confused, because she told him that she only wanted to have sex with him. He kept telling her that if she loved him, she would have sex with his friends.

I told her, if anyone asked her to have sex with their buddies, then they didn't care anything about her. She said that she knew that, but at the time she was trying to prove that she really loved Kenneth and that she would do whatever it took, to prove it to him. That's when he asked her to have sex with his buddies. She said she just wanted Kenneth to care about her the way she cared about him.

The way she was talking, I knew she wasn't telling me everything, so I asked her again, if she had sex with other football players. She looked at the floor and shook her head, yes. Then she said only two others.

So I asked if she used protection, and she said no. She said that Kenneth told her that protection wasn't necessary. He said that football player's sperm count was low, because of the activity and practice they do in a day.

After hearing Michelle say, she had unprotected sex with some of the other football players, I told her that maybe she made the right decision on having the abortion. After all, she wasn't sure if the baby was really for Kenneth and none of the other football players was going to claim the baby either. I couldn't help but to tell her to let this be a lesson learned, because she turned against everyone that cared about her, just to become popular and the only people she was popular with, was the football players. I told her, she was only a football player's girlfriend and that didn't make her popular, it only made her a target.

Time went on and Michelle was hanging with all of our old friends again. She no longer wanted to become popular. She said just having friends that cared about her, was enough for her to live with. I on the other hand, kept her at arm's length along with everyone else.

I've always wanted someone that I could trust, someone I could go to, when I was in need of a shoulder to lean on, but I knew it wouldn't be Michelle. Not after what she had put me through.

There was nothing better, than to have a friend to share your secrets, when you knew you couldn't trust anyone else. Friendship is something sacred. You can't call every person you meet a friend. A friend is someone that's proud of you, not jealous of your accomplishments. A friend is a person that will be there for you for whatever the reason may be. A friend is someone you don't have to communicate with every day. You don't even have to communicate every week, but when you need that friend. That friend will always be there for you, with no questions asked. A friend is also a person that you can tell your most valuable secrets to, and you don't ever have to worry about hearing that secret being told to anyone else. A friend is also hard to find, so if you ever come cross someone that you can consider a friend, hold on to their friendship forever, because a true friend last forever and always.

In my life time, I can say that I've had four people in my life that I can truly call a friend. Three of them only communicate with me when they have time and I understand that, because I'm the same way. Things change as life goes on and so do we, but our friendship is always the same.

Sometimes we go years without communicating, but when I need them or they need me, there are no questions asked. It's as if time sat still and we are right back where we needed to be, and that's in each other's lives with no strings attached.

They are always there for me and vise versa. I don't have to worry about them thinking, I forgot about them or I no longer have time to for them. When we do talk, we have a lot to say and so much to catch up on, which makes the conversation even better.

Chapter 2

Family Drama

It's sad when you have to put your own family members at arm's length, just to keep the peace and savage the relationship. Arm's length was the only way I could save my relationship with certain family members. I'm not good at hiding my true feelings, because my attitude shows on my face. It's hard for me to pretend everything is okay when I know it not. I'd rather be somewhere else, doing something that I like to do, with people that I want to be with.

My mother was good at keeping family drama at its peak. Being a country woman, she loved to cook, so she would cook up a good Sunday meal and have her entire family come over. It was as if she had radar senses that detected when we had a problem with each other. She would strike up positive conversations that would make us all forget about whatever it was we were disagreeing up on, and think about how we've grown and overcame a lot of discomforts by sticking together. It wouldn't be long before everyone was at the dinner table, eating and sharing their own version of their side of the stories, my mother would come up with.

Our biggest problems were at family reunions. No matter how many times a year the family tried to come together, there would always be a fight with someone's family. Someone would disagree with another family member and before you know it, a big fight would turn out. Minutes later, another family member would jump in, to take up for one of the family members that were already fighting and another family member would jump in, and so on. Soon afterwards the police would be involved and there goes the family reunion.

One year my uncle was very upset with my stepfather, because my stepfather grabbed my sister by the arm. My uncle told my stepfather he had no right to grab my sister in that manner. My stepfather, not knowing what he was about to get into, told my uncle to mind his own business. My uncle, which was my stepfather's brother, ran up to my stepfather and grabbed him like he grabbed my sister. To defend himself my stepfather grabbed his brother by the neck and pushed him to the ground. When another uncle of mind saw this incident, he ran over and grabbed my stepfather.

Not knowing who had grabbed him. My stepfather hit his other brother in the face. The hit was so forceful. It knocked my uncle to the grown. My aunt began screaming and that made things even worst. She was married to my uncle that my stepfather pushed to the ground. When her brother heard her screaming, he thought my stepfather hit my aunt. He pulled out a gun and started shooting at my stepfather, because he saw him standing in a rage position with both fist raised in the air. He missed my stepfather and shot one of my uncles in the stomach twice. Somehow the police got to the scene before the ambulance, and my stepfather was taken to jail. I don't know what was said for the police to take my stepfather and not my aunt's brother, because it was my aunt's brother that did all the shooting.

The truth never came out that day and my stepfather spent a year in jail, behind something that was uncalled for. He was minding his own business, taking care of a problem that happened between him and his daughter that somehow got out of hand. His brother had no reason to interfere with how my stepfather was disciplining his child, but my uncle didn't want my stepfather causing a scene at the family reunion. He wanted this to be the first reunion without drama. But instead, he made it the worse family reunion ever.

I remember watching my aunt hold my uncle's intestines in with both hands, until the ambulance arrived. All the younger children were crying while their parents tried covering their faces. My uncle survived the shooting and my other uncle was forgiven by the rest of the family, for starting the incident. I heard rumors of why my stepfather went to jail in his brother's place. His brother had previous encounters with the police and was on parole, so my stepfather took the blame for shooting his brother and served a year in jail for self defense. They were a very close family with multiple family problems. But when push came to shove, they always had each other's back.

When my stepfather was released from jail everything went back to normal, as if nothing ever happened. There wasn't a year, when the family didn't have to fight. Every year the fights got worst, so after the shooting incident the reunions stopped. Family members were getting beaten, stabbed and even shot. The younger family members began to lose respect for the older family members, it was a shame how the family didn't get along, but had a bond thick as stone.

People were jealous of other families and would steal from them, knowing other people in the family were going to tell. Some family members were so good at telling lies, they would look you straight in the eyes while lying and you couldn't get them to tell the truth if their lives depended on it. Family members were dating each other. We had stepsisters and brothers having babies together and half sisters and brothers dating each other. Not to mention, cousins dating cousins. There was no secret as to who was dating who or who dated the person first. Kids were being born with mental issues and family members would tell the kids they were crazy, because their parents were relatives. Before the day was over, a fight would start.

The drama had gotten so bad one year, two family members were shot and six people were sent to jail. One family member accused his brother of cheating with his wife and when the wife tried to break up the fight, she got shot in the butt by the man she was cheating with. She was rushed to the hospital and neither of the brothers visited her. When she was released from the hospital, she went home to an empty house and the brothers moved on with their lives.

Things were so crazy with the family. The only way to keep peace and out of confusion was to put most of the family at arm's length. There were too many secrets that the family wanted to keep between the older family members.

It was as if the family wanted the drama, because every year fights broke out for no apparent reason. Some of the family members said they wanted to know about the secrets that were going on in their lives, and some said they didn't care less about the secrets. My point of the matter was to keep them all at arm's length and go on with my life.

Why have a secret with family members if you know it's going to be told?

Especially when you know your family is not trust worthy. You do better telling the secret yourself, and it would cut out a lot of confusion. But that's only my opinion. I've always tried to make things right with people. I never liked confusion. I tried my best to stay as far away from trouble, as I possibly could.

It really hurts when someone you truly love turns their back on you, for something you know nothing about. I was very close to one of my older brothers, but for some apparent reason, he turned his back on me and didn't have anything to say to me. I didn't know why, so I decided to put him at arm's length, until he was ready to come to me. Finally, about two months later, at one of our family Sunday dinners with our mother, I found out that my cousin told my brother, I was the reason his wife left him. I was very close to my brother and his wife and I knew she was going to leave him. But I wasn't the reason she left. She had grown out of love with my brother and she talked to me about it. She was confused at the time, because my brother was her first love, but my brother became distant with her. He was doing some of the things he used to do with her, at the beginning of the marriage, but she could tell he wasn't into the excitement like he used to be.

He hid the fact of dating other women. He had done nothing to make her feel like he was cheating, but she had her instincts, so she decided to leave him.

She met and fell in love with a much younger guy that liked doing the things she enjoyed doing. This younger guy made her feel special. She said he made her feel young again. My brother was a womanizer. He loved women and one woman wasn't enough for him. He knew he had a good wife, he just didn't like doing the things she liked doing, because it took up too much of his time. He never tried to stop her from doing the things she liked doing, because he knew she enjoyed doing them. But she wanted him to enjoy her fun times with her and he just couldn't do it anymore. The fun just wasn't there for him.

My sister-in-law was determined to find that spark again, so she began to go out alone. While she was having fun doing the things she liked doing. She met a nice young man to share her time with. He was four years younger than her and he liked older women. Neither of them had any kids, so that made it easier for them to meet whenever necessary. My sister-in-law didn't mean to fall in love with this younger guy, but he really made her feel special, whenever they were together. She found herself wanting to be with him more and more, but she knew it wasn't right, because she had a husband at home that was good to her, but her husband refused to put her first.

It was a battle at first, but her heart really went out for the younger guy. My brother never thought his wife would cheat on him, because they had such a good relationship. They had always trusted each other and he had no idea, another man was involved with his precious jewel. My sister-in-law didn't know how to love two men at once, because my brother was her first. Things were beginning to get out of hand, and she didn't know how to choose between the two men.

She knew of our family history. So she didn't trust a lot of our family members. I was one of the people in the family that she felt comfortable talking to.

So when she came to me, to tell me about her situation. I took it serious. She had been with my brother for nine years and they were married for five. I tried telling her, that she was going through something that happens to most women that has been with one man, for such a long period of time and now she wants to try something different.

My brother was her first, so naturally she sees something different in this young man. Instead of telling her to pray about her situation, I told her to test the waters and see if she really wanted to give up the love of her life, of nine years. I guess I told her what she wanted to hear, because she gave me a hug, a kiss on the cheek and told me thank you.

We never talked about her, my brother or the young man ever again. In less than a year, she left my brother and moved in with her younger friend.

She and my brother never divorced, so I thought they talked about what she was going through and decided to separate, to sort thing out. My brother never had anything to say to me after my sister-in-law moved out. He would walk right pass me and wouldn't say a word. I would speak to him and he would look me straight in the eyes and walk away. I knew it had something to do with my sister-in-law, but I didn't know what. I wasn't sure if my sister-in-law told him, she talked to me and I encouraged her to leave him, or if she told him she talked to me before leaving him.

I didn't want to seem guilty of something I didn't do, but I didn't know how or what to say to my brother about the situation. I know he loved his wife very much and he put her on a pedestal. He would have never in a million years, thought his wife would leave him for another man. He tried to do everything right in her eyes to hold on to her, because she was a good woman. They both had a lot in common and they chose together to wait to have kids, so they could do all the things they wanted to do and spend good quality time with their children whenever the time would come.

But the time would never come now, because she is with another man and they seemed to be happy. Other family members tried talking to my brother, to get him to give up other women and get his wife back, because they could see the unhappiness in his eyes. Being without his wife was hard. No one ever saw this side of him. He loved all women. We always known his wife was special, because he married her. No one ever thought he would get married, because of his love for different types of women.

When he found his wife, she was a virgin with a good hurt and a great personality. My brother saw a chance to make the woman of his life, out of this one particular woman. He thought he could mold her to be the woman of his dreams. He wanted to train her to please him in every way possible, so he wouldn't need another woman, but it didn't work out that way.

I really didn't know if my brother was accusing me of destroying his marriage, but it sure seemed like it. My family kept so much drama going on. I just didn't know how to go to my brother and ask him if what I heard was true. After all, it was my family I was dealing with and rumors could spread fast. I didn't know if my cousin actually talked to my brother, or if this was just another rumor that was going around.

How would my cousin know about the conversation I had with my sister-in-law anyway?

We both were living on an after fact, going by what someone else had told us. The look in his eyes, when he looked at me, seemed to tell me all that I needed to know. I got butterflies in my stomach, just thinking about how my brother thought I was the cause of him losing his wife.

I was told, my brother regrets not having any children with his wife and seeing his nieces and nephews playing well with each other, seemed to make him even more disappointed. He continues to come to the family gatherings, but he keeps everyone at arm's length.

I had a cousin that I liked hanging out with at the gatherings, but she turned against the family when she found out her husband was having an affair with another cousin of ours. I knew about the affair, but I didn't think it was up to me, to tell my cousin. I didn't want to be the cause of any misunderstandings. Some people don't take bad news as well as you would think they would take it, and since I wasn't sure of what her reactions would be. I put everyone in that circle at arm's length.

I know my family, and confusion is something that seems to keep them in touch with one another. My cousin called me on the phone and asked me what I thought of the situation she and her husband was going through and I kept my decisions to myself. I told her, I had my own problems and she had to sit down and talk to her husband about what really happened, because he was the only one that could tell her what she needed to know. I told her to stop putting the family into her private situations and work things out with her husband. In the end, she was the one that had to deal with the situation, so she needed to keep whatever was going on between them in a circle of people that she trusted, because our family couldn't be trusted.

I told her that I don't believe that there is a perfect family. Everyone has some type of secret or problem, but they know how to keep their secrets and problems within their own circle, to keep other people out of their business.

She began to wonder why I kept my distance from everyone. But I didn't have the heart to tell her the truth, so I told her to sit back and think about all the things our family goes through. If she would just think of all the drama and problems that goes on with our family, she would see that it all starts with some type of rumor, from a family member which started a long time ago. Our family has been going through drama for years and it's not about to stop now. So put most of our family at arm's length and have peace in her marriage.

I'm the type of person, who likes to see everyone getting along well with each other. I'm not good with confusions and mishaps. I'd rather stay away than to face drama. I guess in every family there's someone who likes to stir up trouble, and if you are anything like me. Try to keep that person at arm's length. You'll find out how misery loves company.

Chapter 3

That Don't Make It Right

There are some people that you just can't tell anything. It's sad when a person takes a positive conversation, and for no apparent reason, turns the conversation into something drastic and meaningless. And when you try to address the issue, other people would try to justify the problem by saying: (Don't pay her any attention, because she's always been that way.)

This person is my sister and she constantly causes mishaps with everyone in the family. She would add a word, or simple subtract a word from a sentence to make herself, look good in another person's eyes. She always wants the attention focused on her, and she would do anything to get that attention, no matter whose life is destroyed to make her accomplishment.

She wants to be the run to person, and in order for that to happen, she has to destroy the relationship of others, so they would run to her for advice. This is a person that everyone should always keep at arm's length.

She carries the behavior of a sociopath, which is a person that has no sense of conscious toward others. She could portray to others, as if she was a perfect angel. But she's only trying to get the trust of anyone that would listen to her. Just to be taken advantage of later, because she has no heart. Sometimes, I wonder if she realizes the pain she causes other people. She only thinks about herself and what she could get from others.

Other family members knows my sister has always had this problem and they always tries to protect her by saying, she don't mean any harm, but the harm is there and that don't make it right. Everyone should be accounted for his or her actions, because every action causes a reaction. So if there is someone in your life that causes problems, every time he or she comes around, maybe it time for you to do the obvious thing, and put that person at arm's length.

My sister has to be the center of attention. If she don't get the attention that she feels she should have, she would pretend to be sick, make herself throw up, trip and fall or even admit herself into the hospital for a couple of days, just to get special attention. But for whatever the reason she does these things, that don't make it right. She's going to find herself in some mental ward, if she continues to do the things that she does.

No one wants to be around someone that constantly has to have special attention. It's okay once in a while, but all of the time is pretty unusual. I believe my sister had played this sick game so much. She has convinced herself that she is really sick. She keeps going back and forth to the hospital and gets turned away, because doctors can't find anything wrong with her. She's like the little boy that cried wolf. She's lied so much, no one believes her when she is telling the truth.

She's going to find herself all alone one day and something is going to happen to her, and no one is going to believe her.

Really, who wants to be sick?

There's nothing good about being sick. I think that she has caused so much confusion with people, the only way anyone would come to visit her is if she is admitted into the hospital, or is confined to a bed and can't get up. But family members always have some kind of excuse for her, as if what she is doing is right. Personally, I can't stand it, and to make everyone else happy, I keep her at arm's length.

When I think of all the drama she has caused in the family and everyone says to look over what she does, because that's the way she is, all I can say is that don't make it right. She has been doing the same thing for too many years and she knows what she is doing is wrong.

So why look over it?

If we confront her with the lies and crazy games she's playing, maybe she'll stop. Sometimes I think, she thinks we are as crazy as she is, for putting up with her. No one in their right minds would do the things my sister does and get away with it for as long as she has. She has destroyed relationships, marriages, friendships and families, with the stupid games she plays and I really thinks she sit back and laugh at us, for letting her get away with the things she does.

My mother's brother had been on heroin for a long time. He was in the military for a while and was diagnosed with schizophrenia. After serving eight years of service, he was granted an honorable discharge release. His drug habit progressed as time went on, and he began to take things from the family to support his drug habit. Most of the family paid him no attention. They just let him do whatever was necessary to help him, support his drug habit, because it made things easier. But that don't make it right. At family gatherings, my uncle would take money out of family member's purses and steal valuable out of houses.

People would turn their head and look the other way, as if what my uncle was doing was right. My nieces would hide their purses in the trunk of their cars and take off any fancy jewelry, because my uncle would always ask if he could have whatever he thought he could get money for. Again, that don't make it right.

I refused to put away my jewelry and I would tell my uncle no, he couldn't have what was in my purse and he couldn't take the jewelry off of my neck. My grandfather would tell me to calm down, he would say, I know my uncle had a serious problem and he means well. They would rather my uncle take from us, than to steal from others. I told my grandpa, that don't make it right. Instead of letting my uncle have his way, when we know what he is doing is wrong, we need to steer him in the right direction and get him some help.

There were plenty of narcotics rehabs that would accept my uncle. But my family wanted to hide the fact and keep everything in the family. They were trying not to shame the family's name. I told them that the family name was already shamed. People knew about my uncle's condition. It was hard not to have known. The news spread quickly and no one wanted to come around our family, when my uncle was around. It was mainly because my family ignored the problem and let my uncle take things from other people that they knew as well.

People wanted to feel comfortable, when they came over to visit. No one wanted to keep an eye on their things, while my uncle was walking around picking out valuables to trade in for drugs. He needed help and my family wasn't willing to give it to him. I thought of getting him help on my own, but I didn't want the family to turn against me, for trying to do the right thing.

In my uncles own sneaky little way, I really thought, he knew what he was doing. Hell, if I could get away with doing wrong, while people turned and looked the other way, I would do exactly what my uncle was doing. But that don't make it right.

My uncle was once married, and has a son named after him, that we called Junior. He would sometimes act like his father. But the family wouldn't let him get away with his wrong doing. So he would sometimes point things out for his father to take, and then he would take it from him. But they wouldn't take things from me. They thought I was mean, so they would bypass me and my immediate family.

They would take things from another family member that was sitting or standing near me, but they knew not to come my way, because I would embarrass them. If my family members was okay with them taking from them, then so was I. I wasn't there to protect their belongings, because they were the reason, my uncle did the taking of other family member's and friend's valuables.

I would sometimes wonder if my uncle and his wife were one of the relatives that married and had a child together. Their whole immediate family was crazy, including their grandchild. Junior never married, but he had a daughter with a girl that was around the family for a long time. Her family had issues too. So she and Junior really understood each other. He got along well with her people and she did the same, when it came down to our people. I'm not sure why they never married. They act as if they couldn't live without one another and they seemed to get along better, when we had family gatherings. I always thought it was because Junior and his father were stealing things from the rest of the family, to give to their families. No one in my uncle's family worked. Everything they had, was either taken from another family member or given to them, so they could live in comfort.

I guess that would make me get along better with my significant other too, if his family made sure I was living in comfort and didn't have to work for it, but that still don't make it right.

It's amazing how other people can sit back and find fault in other people households, as if their situations are perfect. A person can write a book about someone else's life issues and find no faults at all, when it comes to their own home. But to me, everyone has skeletons. No one is perfect and there's a story to be told with any and every family, whether it's good, bad or scary. There's always a story to be told.

Some families sit back and laugh about their family drama, some people rather hide their family drama and then you have some families, who just don't give a damn. They don't care about their family's issues and they don't care if the world knows about, because it is what it is.

No matter how bad or eccentric my family seems to be, there is always someone else's family in worst conditions. I think it's pretty cool when people accept their outlandish family history and share it with the world. Because what some people call odd and unusual, others find magnetism. I understand when families are ashamed to admit there is a family member that requires special attention and would like to keep it in the family. But if nothing is done to correct that family member's action, it makes the problem worst. You can't just accept the issue and expect things to be okay. That don't make it right. I can think of a lot of things that I feel needs taken care of in my bazaar family.

But if no one has the man power to correct the issues, why complain?

All it takes is for one person to stand up for the entire family, and try to make a difference. Stop pushing thing under the rug, hoping it will work itself out. If it's not seen, that don't mean it's not there. After a while the rug will have a huge lump in it, and the problem will be more noticeable. Now the problem is bigger and probably harder to get rid of.

I say my way of handling things is by putting people at arm's length, and it seems to work for me. But my way might not be the right way, because it's like pushing the problem under the rug and trying to forget about it, but it's still there.

I don't claim to be perfect. I might have family members that are looking at me and saying I'm the problem. They probably see something in me that is strange to them and decide to keep me at arm's length as well. There are some thing that I do are different, but I'm willing to correct the issue, if someone comes up with a good suggestion.

For instance, I have a daughter that's gay and I didn't know how to accept it. It was a hard challenge for me, but on the other hand she's my child and I still love her. I choose not to talk about it and I guess that's my way of pushing my problems under the rug, but that don't make it right. Her partner is a great person and loves my daughter unconditionally. Her partner's parents have no problem with the issue and welcome my daughter into their home, as if she was a child of their own. Unlike them, I asked my daughter to keep her partner at arm's length from me, until I was ready to accept the situation.

The less I saw them together, the more comfortable I was, with the relationship. When I asked my daughter how and why, she said it just happened. She said they were very close friends at first and could talk to each other about anything. But one day her partner was hurt by a boyfriend and came to my daughter to talk about it, and tears began to flow.

So they held each other and shortly, they were kissing. She said it felt right and that's when she knew she liked girls. I tried to tell her, she was just comforting a friend that needed a shoulder to lean on, but she told me no. I was wrong, it was much more than that and she would tell me the same thing each and every time I asked her the question. So I left well enough alone and accepted my daughter as being gay and keep the both of them at arm's length. Because the less I know about their relationship, the better I feel about the situation.

I guess I was more ashamed, than anything else. I didn't want to think about what other people were thinking about, two women being together in a relationship that was meant to be an opposite attraction. Sometimes I sit and wonder if it was my fault.

Did I have one of those crazy babies that my family said was made from sleeping with a relative?

My family was so mixed up. Maybe my husband was a long lost cousin that no one knew about. The reason for our family reunions was to get to know all family members, so the crazy baby rumor would stop. My family wanted everyone in the family to know their family's life history and have no surprise unusual crazy babies.

My aunt's husband doesn't know how to read or write and he can barely count money. She is a stay home mom and manages all the money. She sometimes wondered if her twin daughters would have problems learning, because their father has a hard time trying to learn how to count money. My aunt decided to put some money away, just in case she needed to use it for additional private learning lessons for the twins. There were times when my aunt would go as far, as to pretend she was robbed, so she could put money away for other things. My uncle never found out about my aunt's secret, putting money away in different placing in the house, because he couldn't count anyway. Lots of family members knew of my aunt's secret and no one said anything to my uncle, because they didn't feel like it was any of their concern. They felt that if my uncle took the time to learn how to count money, he could keep up with where his money was going. But of course, I felt like that don't make it right. Just because he couldn't read or count, doesn't give his wife the right to take his hard earned money from him. And to pretend that she was being robbed by a stranger, to put money aside was ridiculous. Because she could have put the money away and not tell my uncle about it, because he couldn't count money that well.

So why go through all the extreme of pretending someone took the money?

My aunt didn't feel comfortable putting the money in a bank, because banks got robbed and she didn't want to have the money she stole, stolen from her. So she kept the money in the house. She never felt guilty about taking the money, because she said my uncle should have learned how to read, write and count when he was younger. She really didn't think it was call stealing, because she said she was putting money away for her twin's future, which made since to me. But that don't make it right.

My uncle signs his name by writing an X and he's pretty good at counting small bills, but when it came to the large bills, he became confused and since my aunt handles all the bills, he had no desire to learn. He strongly trusts his wife. She's going to continue to take from him, because he lost all confidence in himself. My aunt always had an excuse to give to my uncle for the money shortages, because he believed everything she told him.

There were times. She would include her sister into the drama, so they could split the money. Others would sit back and watch as my aunt and her sister robbed my uncle blind. The people that sat and watched agreed with aunt, when she said my uncle should have learned how to manage his own money. But that just don't make it right. My uncle knew he couldn't read or count, that's why he put a lot of trust into my aunt. As for me, I decided to keep my aunt and her sister at arm's length.

I have a cousin that would always get drunk and take friends of hers on joy rides. Everyone in the car would be drinking and playing loud music while swerving around cars, as if it was so much fun. But one time my cousin swerved, one time too many. She was driving drunk and swerved the car around a tree. Everyone in the car was pronounced dead. My cousin was barely alive. She lost an eye, her leg and her arm was hanging on by threads. The doctors worked on her for hours. When they were finally through with her, my cousin looked like the walking dead. She put fear in all the younger kids, in the family. They all were afraid to drink and drive after seeing my cousin's after the fact look.

You would think that having all your friends die, in a car incident that you caused, would stop anyone from wanting to drink and drive again. But my cousin had a death wish. She no longer wanted to live with the guilt. So she continued drinking and driving. Years later, she had another fatal accident. She had to be cut out of the car and she had to have major surgery again. She made it through again. She thought she was invincible, and that nothing could take her life away from her, because she survived two major accidents and lived to tell about.

The most amazing thing about her second accident, the doctors performed hours of surgery on her and found out she was pregnant. The doctors managed to save the baby and six months later, my crippled, one eyed, one leg and one arm, which was turned backward, because that was the only way the doctors could attach the arm back together, drug addict cousin gave birth to a beautiful baby girl. The baby wasn't addicted to the drugs my cousin was using, but she did have some drugs in her system. For the first few months of the baby's life, she cried constantly. I guess, it was because of the drugs.

My cousin's habits had gotten worst and she was now selling sex and robbing the men that she sleeps with. She would put something in the men drinks to put them asleep, while she took their money and left them in the motel room. She was living her life for herself. She cared nothing for her daughter. She didn't even know who the baby's father was and we couldn't figure out who would want to have sex with her, looking the way she looked. But that don't make it right.

She was living on borrowed time and sooner or later, she was going to get what she was trying to achieve. It seemed as if, drug addictions ran in the family, because I can tell some stories that would make you cry.

I have an uncle that started smoking weed with his daughter, because he didn't want her to sneak out with friends and start doing drugs. He thought if he would introduce her to the drugs first, by starting her off with the small stuff, she would only smoke with him. But things didn't go as he planned.

My cousin didn't want her father to know how much she really liked smoking weed. She was not only smoking with him, but she was also smoking with whomever she could get in contact with. By hiding her addiction from her dad, she began to smoke crack and then she moved up to something called wet. Now wet is weed dipped in embalming fluid. The wet made her hallucinate, but she really liked the way it made her feel.

By the time her father found out about her addiction. It was too late. She was too far gone. He blamed himself for his daughter's drug addiction, because he was the one that started her to smoking weed. Other family members seemed to agree with him. If he hadn't started her to smoking at such an early age, with him, then she wouldn't be in the predicament that she was in. But that don't make it right.

Instead of introducing his daughter to drugs, he should have sat down and talked to her about drugs and explained to her how addictive drugs can become.

I always thought drugs, cigarettes, and drinking was a mind game. It's all up to you and how you look at things in life. You have absent minded people, who try things just because someone else says it okay. You also have people that are insecure, that try things without thinking. They let someone else do the thinking for them and before they know it. They are hooked on something and don't know how to stop on their own.

These are the people that dope dealers prey on to make their money and that don't make it right. It's happening every day and becoming a huge circle of life.

Life is like a box of chocolates. You'll never know what's inside until you take a bite and believe it or not, my family is that box of chocolate coated candy and that don't make it right.

Chapter 4

Keeping Your Distance

Sometimes I get lonely, because I was used to having my family and friends around me. But I feel it's necessary to keep the peace by staying away and only come around if I was needed. This way, I knew what was needed of me. I would do no more or no less than what was asked to do. I knew where I stood, because I kept my distance and there shouldn't be any type of conflict, as to why I was there.

When you're around people that likes to fight all the time or constantly using profanity to prove they are bigger and better than others. It's best to just keep your distance. My mother told me that most people that think they can't be beat are either dead or in jail and if they haven't made it there, they were on their way. So I stay clear of those types of people.

It didn't take a rocket scientist to tell me something that made sense to me and you didn't have to tell me twice. I knew right from wrong and the term good from bad. So I always tried to make the best decisions and be an example to others. I tried keeping my distance to things that didn't matter to me. It wasn't so much as staying away from my family and friends, unless I felt uncomfortable with the conversations or vulgar body language indicating something bad was about to happen. I didn't care too much for drama. If in any way possible, I sensed trouble was about to happen, I would keep my distance. I had better things planned for my future and prison time wasn't one of them. I like having fun and doing positive things with positive people. I enjoyed learning to make or build things.

I always thought of being someone well known. So if I was to pass on, I would be well remembered as the person that made a difference. I wanted to be the one that got away. My family was so messed up and confused in the head. They couldn't see life no further than the present. They lived their lives from day to day and it didn't matter if they were living their last day in tragedy and was about to die right there on the spot. It just would have been another day for them.

So I tried to distance myself away from that type of life. I always saw a future for me. My biggest mistake was having too many ideas going on in my head at one time. I would start on one idea and accomplish it, but before I could make it huge and noticeable to the world, I would be starting on something else. I'm not saying having lots of ideas are wrong, because it's not. Actually it's a great idea to have more than one dream. Just complete your dream.

For example: your dream should have a short term and a long term goal. Don't stop with your dream just because you accomplished your short term goal. Continue until your long term dream is accomplished, then start working on your next accomplishment. This way your first dream would have grown passed its peak and can help you with your next dream. Then you wouldn't have to worry about your first accomplishment, because it's doing what you planned for it to do and you can concentrate on your next profitable dream.

If you continue the steps that you did with your first accomplishment, then you would have accomplished another dream come true. Now to stay focus, you must keep your distance from anything or person that's going to hold you back. Sometimes it's going to take for you to feel lost and alone, because you are away from your friends and family, but in the long run, it will be a big accomplishment for you.

People and obstacles can slow down your process, because you won't focus as well as you should be. But if you are surrounded with positive people that will help motivate you. It won't take long to finish what you started. People that mean you no good will talk about you, whether you become successful or fail at your first try, but they have no ideas of their own. They will try anything and everything to keep you down with them. And if you give up on your dream, just to become part of the crowd. It wasn't for you in the beginning. You were only trying to accomplish something to prove a point to either yourself or someone that told you to try it and see what happens.

Keep your distance. Never try out for something if your heart isn't in it. You don't have to prove nothing to anyone, just to see if you'll going to fail trying. Once you put your heart into something, there is no stopping you.

People can tell you all day long, you'll never make it. But you'll continue trying, because it's something you want for yourself and not to prove you can't do it. It's going to mean something to you and that's what's going to keep you focus, motivated and positive. There's nothing wrong with hanging out with negative people. You can get some of your greatest ideas by hanging out with negativity. Negative people always have something to say about someone else. They talk about how they can do it better and some might even come up with a better idea, but they'll never accomplish it. If you was to take their idea and improve it, that's when all hell breaks loose, and you become a thief.

They're going to say, it was their idea first and you stole it. But mind you, they never acted upon the idea. They were just running off at the mouth with no intentions of doing anything. And if you are not careful, you'll let them talk you out of completing your accomplishment. That's why I say, keeping your distance from negative environments is a positive move for the future.

There are positive people that have really good ideas, but they have no one to motivate them to keep the dream going. Just because you don't have the money to start up your idea, doesn't mean you can't continue with the structure. If you surround yourself with positivity, you can find other ways of starting up. Sometimes this might mean you have to start out small and work your way up the latter. Most businesses started out small, but the person that started it, had big dreams and continued working at it, until it became their vision. There are people that have no idea where to start with a business, but being around positive people, helped them to step out on faith. And if there is one thing I know, it's to step out on faith and plenty of positive things will happen for you. You'll have people offering their quality time to help you get started. You'll have people that will work for you for free and people that will volunteer services that are needed to keep your business running. But you have to believe it's going to work. You can't give up, just because things aren't going as you planned. Remember everything takes time. The world wasn't built in one day.

You have to treat your business as if it's a new born baby and watch it grow from that.

A person with a strong business mind is like a loaded gun. If you pull the trigger, it will shoot and there's no telling where the bullet will land. All they know is they are eager and ready to fire. There are so many people out there that are willing to help anyone that is willing to help themselves. You'll be surprised at how many people appreciate individuals that wants to start their own businesses. Some people like helping entrepreneurs, because it reminds them of small mom and pop shops. It takes a lot of guts to step out into the business world and compete with franchised businesses. So this is where your support comes from other entrepreneurs.

You'll have entrepreneurs that wanted to start their business, but just didn't have the faith to step out on, and do what was in their heart, because they had a family to take care of and couldn't go without getting paid. Then you have the entrepreneurs that wanted to start up a business, but didn't have the patient. Because with most businesses, it takes about three years before a profit is seen. For the first three years, all the money that's made through the business, is put back into the business to keep the business flowing. So they would rather help someone else with their business to ease their troubled minds, and it works out for both parties. So if you want to become someone special, just remember to keep your distance from negativity and you'll be alright.

I have to say, I really admire one of my family members for keeping his distance from the family. Due to his courageous move, he has become very successful in life. He tied a knot at the end of his rope and hung on for as long as he could. Dealing with all the family's drama had taken a toll on him and he just wanted something different for his family. When he was at the end of his rope, he decided to tie a knot and hang on to keep from falling deeper and deeper into the family's history of mischief. He decided to keep his immediate family at arm's length, by taking them to a different state. He got as far away from the family as he could and started a new life somewhere else. By leaving one state and entering another, he no longer had any interest in what the family thought about him and his family. He just wanted a new beginning, where no one knew him and he knew no one. He was already at the end of his rope and he could only hold on to that knot for so long, before he would fall into deeper drama.

I had an associate named Jack and he's very intelligent, but he was overweight and had a bad case of acne on his face. Jack would come to work and be finished in three hours, of an eight hour day. During his free time he would read two or three books to kill time. He really enjoyed reading. Sometimes he made me so upset with him, because I knew how smart he was.

What good is it to be smart, with plenty of book sense and have no common sense?

I tried telling him that people were taking advantage of him at work, but he said he didn't mind. He seemed to think they liked him, because they were always smiling in his face. But they talked about him, when his back is turned. When I told him that they do like him, but it's not for the reason he thinks they like him. He asked like he didn't understand.

I think he didn't want to understand, because when he does all the extra work for other employees, they buy him lunch and give him gifts.

I guess if you'll going to be used by someone, it's good to get something out of it as well. It was also a way for him to receive attention and to be noticed.

It just hurt my feelings to see how the other employees got over on him and thought nothing of it. It was like a chain gang going on at his work station.

Other employees were buying him gifts and lunch every day. It was a way for the other employees to pay off their guilt and not have to feel guilty about the way they treated him.

Jack mostly like scratch off tickets, so they would bring him one or two scratch off tickets, in return for hours of hard earned work. It seemed so unfair to me, but Jack was so content with the attention he was getting, so I decided to keep my distant.

People like that, I try to keep my distance and put them at arm's length. These are people that are users and would do anything to get over on someone.

I tried telling Jack that doing other employees work was not fare to him and he should tell them that he no longer wanted to do their work, but he thought he had friends. So I sit back and watched him being taken advantage of, knowing it wrong. I've even said something to the employees that were taken advantage of him and they seemed to think I was jealous.

Shirley Jordan

I knew Jack wasn't happy doing other people's work. But he was overweight, felt uncomfortable with his appearance, didn't have any friends outside of the job and was good at his work skills. So I guess he was using them in a way too. He got the attention that he wanted, at the cost of a scratch off ticket. Jack seemed to be a person that grew up alone, and it paid off. He studied very hard and read lots of books to make up for the loneness.

I continued to talk to him about the way he chooses his friends, and hopefully one day he will realize how special he is. He don't have to do things for others that makes him unhappy, just to make someone like him, because in the end, they are only using him and that's not fair to either of them. I told him, he was only teaching the other employees how to take advantage of other people that might have the same issue that he has. And that won't be fair for the next person either.

They were getting paid to do the work that he was doing for them and he wasn't getting any of the credit, besides a couple of scratch off tickets that they would purchase for him.

I didn't want him to feel bad about the way he was going about making friends, but those types of friends was good for no one.

I just wanted him to know he was better than that and the other employees were wrong for taking the easy way out at work. They were doing what they wanted to do, while Jack did all of their work.

He told me he had kept his distance from people for so long, because of his appearance. He just wanted someone other than his family to notice him. Since he was so fast at what he was doing and had the extra time, he felt it was okay to do the other employees work.

In his mind, it made him feel special and he knew it was wrong, but he refused to go back to spending his extra time reading books that he had already read more than twice. Having someone using him was a lot less depressing, than having someone not noticing him at all. To him this was a step closer to learning how to communicate with others and except the way he looked.

He had distanced himself from people, because he had no self esteem. He knew he was good at reading and he could catch on to things pretty quick. But because of his appearance, he was afraid of not fitting in with others.

So after hearing that, I decided to keep my distant and put not only Jack, but the other employees that were taking advantage of him, at arm's length. Because I knew that there was nothing else I could do about the situation.

Sometimes it good to step back and let things take its course, so you can learn if it's your place to stop what's going on and live with the decision that was made.

Just because I felt uncomfortable with Jack's situation, doesn't mean he had to feel bad about the way he was handling his problem.

So maybe this was a lesson learned for me, to put my distance act in place as well. After all, I was no super saver hoe any way.

Chapter 5

It Is What It Is

When you know you have someone in your life that continuously lies and make up stories. Then you know, it is what it is. Keep yourself at arm's length with that person and soon you will gradually disappear from map and people will began to see you, for whom and what you are. This will make you different from the rest of the people you were used to hanging with and of course, they are going to say some bad things about you.

But if the people you were hanging around didn't have something good to say about you, then you weren't worth hanging with any way. Stop trying to prove yourself to people, because it is what it is. If your family and friends don't realize the person that you are or the person you've been, then you should realize they don't want to see who you really are.

Don't be afraid to shine. If there is something inside of you that is waiting to get out, then open up and show the world. Because it is what it is and a person can either accept it or give it away, either way it's been released and now you will have it out in the opening.

If you've been holding in something that you wanted to say to someone, but just don't know how they will take the news. Let it out, because holding it in will make you so miserable inside, until one day you will explode and its going to come out the wrong way and you'll probably never forgive yourself for the way you released the pressure that you held in for so long.

But once it's out, it is what it is and you'll feel much better about the situation. Sometimes we bring problems upon ourselves. We try so hard to find an easy way to let people know about bad news or news that we know they just don't want to hear. We can't save everybody from bad news, it is what it is and the way they take the news is strictly up to that person.

I have an associate that's been in my life for a long time. She has no children, a good paying job, a nice home, a live in boyfriend and a lot of debt due to credit cards and gambling. She has no money saved and she's living from check to check. Now to her, this is fine because she's handling her business by paying everything on time. But when I tried talking to her about changing her situation and lifestyle, she didn't want to hear what I had to say. She said if she needed my advice, she would come to me and ask for it. I accepted her decision and decided to leave well enough alone and let her do her own thing, because whatever she was doing, it was working out for her.

Who was I to try and change her lifestyle?

The way she was living was working out well for her. Just because I was living my life totally different, doesn't mean she was living her life wrong. I decided to put her at arm's length, because you can't help someone that doesn't want to be helped.

Her live in boyfriend got tired of struggling, but she would always belittle him, by saying he wants to live like the Jones. Whenever he would bring up the subject of them not having extra money saved, always put her into a horrible rage. He didn't like arguing, so he would let well enough alone.

The both of them had good paying jobs, so they should at least have some extra money to spend on other things besides bills. He tried talking to her about giving up gambling, so they could do something together with the money, like a nice trip together. My associate didn't want her boyfriend trying to control her money that she worked hard for every week. She told him if he didn't like the way things were going, then he needed to leave. He didn't want to leave, but he thought, if he left she would probably miss him and give up gambling. While she was gambling off her money every week, he was paying all the bills with his money. He knew, if he was to leave, she wouldn't be able to pay all the bills and have extra money for gambling. So he said fine and packed his things. He thought she would stop him before he reached the door, but she didn't. Her ego was too high for that. He didn't have too many choices to choose from, but he knew he had to make a move. He thought it would be the only way to win his old high school lover back. They had been friends for so long. He couldn't believe that she would chose gambling over him.

He chose to move in with his brother, but it wasn't a wise chose at all. His brother loved partying and most of his money went on booze and strippers. He had a fetish with women sliding down poles and he didn't mind paying the price for his enjoyment.

Without the help of her live in boyfriend, my associate began to have a strong melt down. She didn't have the extra money that he brought to the table. She couldn't gamble without over spending the money to pay the bills. She decided to call her creditors and ask for an increase on the cards she accumulated with her boyfriend. She always paid her bills on time and she had a good paying job, so she was granted the increase on three of her major credit cards.

I decided to go back on my rules of, leaving well enough alone. I tried talking to her again, but this time, I told her she shouldn't have gotten the increase on the credit cards, because the interest rate was going to eat up her money. She took my advice as a gambling joke. She said, it is what it is and she knew what she was doing. So once again, I left well enough alone. It wasn't my place to tell the grown ass woman, how to manage her money.

When the bills started coming in from the credit cards, she called me crying. She said, she couldn't get in touch with her boyfriend and she was behind on her mortgage. I didn't want to say, I tried to tell you so, but it came out any way. I tried to get her to put some money away for hard times, but she thought she had everything under control. She was so busy living from day to day and not for the future. And her excuse was, it is what it is.

All she was doing was digging a hole deeper and deeper. She didn't want to get rid of the lifestyle that she was used of living. I knew where her boyfriend worked, so I went by to see how he was holding out. I asked if he could meet me over to their house, so we could come up with a plan to get the both of them back on their feet.

He agreed to meet me, because he wasn't happy living with his brother. He was paying just as much money living with his brother, than he was paying living with his girlfriend. When we met at the house, I had my associate to put all the bills on the dining room table. I had no idea her gambling habit was as bad as it was. She was spending more money at game rooms and casinos, than she was paying on her credit cards and her mortgage. If it hadn't been for us putting all the bills on the table in front of her, so she could see why she was so behind in her mortgage, she wouldn't have believed it herself.

She was paying below minimum on her credit cards and that caused her to have late payments, which caused her credit cards payments to be higher. Her boyfriend didn't know she called and asked for an increase on the credit cards and this was over the top for him. Right then he decided to give up on the relationship and go solo. He said that he could do badly all by himself. He didn't need help to do badly. He said, he moved in with his brother, so he could save money for them to get back on their feet. But moving out made things worse for them and he refused to live like a poor person, with the amount of money he brought home a week.

With tears in her eyes, my associate didn't know how much money she was blowing off and now that she has lost the only one that could help her climb out of the hole, that she had dug so deeply, she didn't know what to do.

I asked if she was willing to get help, because I didn't think she could quit cold turkey. Her boyfriend told her that he would go with her and stay by her side, because he felt as if it was his fault. He said he knew how much she was gambling off every week, but he didn't say anything, because she was the bread winner in the house, and she would always say: (It is what it is,) when he tried to talk to her about her gambling.

Nothing last forever, we all have our ups and downs, but it's how you handle it, that makes the difference. Some people are stronger than others, which make it easier to handle certain problems when they occur. Some people can't handle pressure at all and will choose to die, instead of working out the issue. In this life that we are living in today, you have to be able to take the bitter with the sweet, the ups with the downs and the good with the bad. We all love sunny days but we have to be able to stand the rain also, because it is what it is.

I never gave up on my associate and her boyfriend, but I didn't want to over stand my boundaries, so I kept them at arm's length and waited until they asked for my help. We all have to learn from our mistakes, because without mistakes how would we know if we are doing good or bad in life. Sometimes you might find yourself going around and around in circles, until you finally figure out what you were doing wrong. Then you see yourself going in a different direction and things began to look better. Life is full of challenges, but you can't be afraid to test the water. It is what it is, you have to be able to take a chance in life or you'll never know what's out there for you.

I can agree and say all things aren't good, but how would you know, if you are afraid to find out what's out there for you. Everyone has to crawl before they walk and just like that baby learning to take that first step, it takes a lot of practice. You would never know if you didn't try. So we have to put ourselves in that baby's position and take a leap of faith on life, because it is what it is.

If you sit back and think about life's beginnings. You could see yourself telling the baby to come on, you can do it and the baby not knowing fear believes he or she can do it. So he or she makes that first step and enjoys the praises we give to them, just because they believed in themselves and took that first step to please us. It's amazing how we take thing in life for granted, until it's no longer there for us.

Then we want to ask the question, why?

We don't want to accept the fact that, it is what it is or you get what you get so don't through a fit. If everyone had to work hard to receive different pleasures in life, this would be a small generation. That's like saying, if men had to give birth to children, there would probably be one child per family if any at all.

Life's no bowl of cherries. The challenges of life are found by different people acknowledging what they can do, and some are found by mistake. But it's not by hanging around negativity, or by thinking, it is what it is. Believe it or not, most inventions were made by mistakes.

My brother was a heavy drug addict. It took a while, but I finally convinced him to seek help. The place where he checked himself into was some place that should have been torn down. The people that were running the place, looked as if they were on drugs or was just completing a drug program themselves. There was no supervision and people were everywhere, doing anything they wanted to do. My brother fitted right in. He didn't see what I saw. I asked him to look for another halfway house somewhere else, but he felt right at home at his new place.

Not long after he moved in, he met a crack head girl living in the same building. It didn't take her long to turn my brother on to the drugs she was using. They began to hang out on street corners, because the place where they were living had no curfews. Everyone was considered grown. So they did whatever they wanted to do, without any consequences. The people that were over the home didn't care if the people that were there for help got the help they needed or not.

I did notice a handful of people that really wanted to get better. The group was in the waiting area playing cards and drinking water. This handful of people had been around so much negativity all their lives. They decided that they had enough. They wanted something better for themselves and this place was the only place that would accept them into their community home, at a price that they could pay.

This place didn't judge them for being down on their luck. They had hit rock bottom, and they now had a room with a bed to sleep in, and three meals a day. This place was a blessing to them and they made a promise to each other, to stick together and make something positive out of their lives.

They were each other's back bone. When one of them started to slip or go backwards, another one would step up and pull that person out of the fire and back to reality. They came up with a system that worked for all of them. And keeping away for all the negativity and wrong doing was hard work. But they knew if they could live in all the pressure and the attempting surroundings that they were in, for the six months lease, without getting into any trouble. Then they could make it in the real world again with a fresh start.

They actually thought living in this awful place was a blessing for them, because they were around all kinds of drugs and alcohol and they had the strength to say no to any wrong doing and hold their heads up high, as the others talked about them. This group was really special to me, because I saw them put themselves at arm's length with the other drug addicts that were only looking for another hand out.

They wanted to get ahead and make a change in their lives for the better. I'm not telling you to turn against anyone, but if they mean you no good, you should think about where you want to be in life. So if you have to put yourself at arm's length to accomplish something, go for it, because it is what it is and that's a fact.

As for my brother, he spent his six months getting high with the new love of his live. I tried talking to him. I wanted him to hang out with the handful of positive people that I met, while I was coming to visit him. He hadn't improved at all. Instead, he had gotten worse. The girl that he met at the home had somehow won his heart, and it wasn't for the better.

He told me that he asked the girl that he met, to marry him and she said yes. I told him that it wasn't a good idea. He told me that she was the best lover that he had ever had. I told him that she was on the streets for a long time, selling her body for drugs. I said she had a lot of practice. So of course she would be a good lover. But he didn't want to hear what I had to say. He began to turn his back on me, because I didn't approve of his wife to be.

The last thing I wanted was for my brother to turn his back on me. So I tried to accept the love of his life. I knew what she was all about and I knew of the life she'd lived. So when she went out on the streets selling her body, so she and my brother could get high together. I just turned the other cheek and pretended I knew nothing. Because it was, what it was and there were no changing things.

My brother's six months was up at this so call rehab building, so he and his wife to be. moved in together with her oldest son. Her son did more drugs than my brother and his mother put together. Like his mother, he was also selling his body for drugs. While they were out making extra money on the streets, my brother stayed home cooking and cleaning. He was a great cook and he never had to stoop so low as to sell his body for anything.

They had a system and it was working out for all of them. I loved my brother very much and I could see his future turning out to be nothing but trouble. But he didn't want to know about his future. He was living for the present and in his eyes, the present was working out just fine for him. He and his wife to be decided to get married, but he didn't want any of his family to attend the wedding celebration. They went to the court house and had a party at their place afterwards.

A year or so into the marriage, my brother found out his wife had AIDS. She had known about the disease long before they got married. He wanted to kill himself. Now he wanted to listen to what I had to say. I told him if he had been having unprotected sex with his wife, then there's a strong possibility that he had the disease as well. He was too afraid to go to the doctor, to see if he was diagnosed with the disease. He thought about all the other men and women that his wife was sleeping with.

What about their partners and the partners after them and so on?

He decided to put his wife and her son at arm's length, so he could get his life in order. He found another organization that was willing to accept him and help him with his drug addiction.

This home was much better than the first community center he went to. They watched their patients closely. This place had zero tolerance and the tenants couldn't have any felonies. If they found out the people living in their community center was doing wrong. The organization would dismiss that person from the center. This place had a ten o'clock curfew and they were very strict about the rules being broken. My brother never told the organization about the possibility of him having AIDS. He said, he was there to get better and telling people that he was a candidate for AIDS wasn't anyone's concern. He said, it is what it is and telling someone about it wouldn't change what he had to live with. He just didn't want people to look at him in a different way. He was more afraid of being rejected from people if they found out he had the disease, because of how he treated people that he knew had AIDS. After all he turned away from the best lover he ever had, because of the disease.

It's sad my brother had to find out he could be sick with a death threatening disease, before he got serious about getting himself together. I just hate it took him to find out his wife was sick, before he decided to get help. My brother and I were very close before he met his wife. She changed him. He was willing to turn away from his entire family, because of the love he had for her. So when he found out she had deceived him, by holding back the truth of her passed illness. He didn't know how to come forward and apologize to his family. His whole attitude about the matter was it is what it is. Now those words are the words to die for.

I knew from the beginning, the girl wasn't right for him. He was trying to leave the drug life and she pulled him deeper into the hole. He had buried himself so deep into the hole, he couldn't climb out. His wife showered him with sex in a way that no woman had ever showed him. I wanted to put my brother at arm's length, but I couldn't, because he wasn't himself. But I was able to keep my distance. He was a grown man and he chose the bed that he wanted to sleep in. He just didn't know that bed had a death wish in it.

My brother stayed at the community center for eighteen months. They helped him find a job and a place to live. He was back to his old self. His clothes were neatly starched, his fingernails were nice and clean and he smelled good. He signed a one year lease with the apartment complex and as long as he was drug free, he had a job to keep his apartment. There was no reason for him to fall flat on his face again. The community center, the apartment complex and his job, all worked together to help people like my brother to get back on their feet, to make a better lifestyle for themselves.

I was very thankful for the help the center gave my brother. I would go by and talk to the people at the center, just to let them know how appreciative I was for the change in my brother. They said it was all my brothers doing. They said, he was ready for a change and they just happen to be there for him, when he became ready.

I never mentioned to my brother how stupid I thought he was for not thinking of the consequences he was making, letting his wife sleep with other people and not knowing someone could bring AID's to their circle.

But it is what it is and we can't change it now, so we all came to his rescue, because it took the three letter word to change my brother's life and become the brother we all loved and remembered.

Chapter 6

Live for Yourself, Not for Others

When you put people that you love at arm's length, it's not saying that you don't care about them. It only states that you chose to live for yourself, not others. You no longer want the drama that follows behind the negative people that are in your life. You've been there and done that. So now it's time for something new.

Living for yourself and not others simple means, you shouldn't have to change who you are, to get alone with other people. If a person can't accept you for who you are or what you've become, just put them at arm's length until they work themselves up to your level. Never down grade yourself or accept less than what you want out of life. I always say, the sky is the limit and that's a long reach, so I'm still reaching because I haven't gotten there yet.

Growing up, I tried living for others and it made me unhappy. But when I gave up on pleasing others and accepted the challenges of having more, it made me proud of myself, because I did it for me and I liked what I was doing.

For the longest time I lived my life's wealth, trying to please a man. But as time went on, I decided to live for me. And if things didn't turn out right, there was no one to blame but myself.

Once others saw the things I was accomplishing, they wanted to get aboard my train. It was a train of love, happiness and freedom. Free to do all the things you desire, without being belittled or let down by trying to live your life for someone else.

Others might have you live the dreams that they couldn't accomplish, and it might not be what you want. So if you feel that you're living someone else's life's dream. So they can see themselves in you. Then you are not going to succeed, and if you do succeed in living someone else life's dream.

Is it really what you want?

Are you just being a puppet on a string to make someone else happy?

Sometimes it takes us to finish a dream for someone else, before we can concentrate on our self. We try so hard to please other people, so we can gain their respect and hopefully get their blessing to finally do what we want to do.

But when a parent had a dream that they couldn't accomplish, they seem to push that dream on their children. What that parent couldn't get when they were younger, they now want their child to get it for them. And that's fine if that's what the child wants to do, but if that child have a different dream, the parent should respect that child's dream.

Don't try to live your life through your child. You missed out. Let your children live their life for them, not for you. It becomes a circle for the next generation. When that child grows up and missed out on his dream, he's going to look for his dream in his child and his child is going to do the same thing and so on, until someone recognizes what they are doing is wrong. So let it go, because it is what it is.

When I was younger I wanted to become a famous singer, actress and a model. But my parents never invested in me. So when I had a daughter, I tried to live my dream through her. I put her in acting and modeling schools, she had private voice lessons. I even had her to take dance and piano lessons. I thought she was happy doing all these things, but when she was old enough to talk to me, she told me all the things I had her doing was for me. She didn't mind doing the things I had her doing at the time, but it wasn't something that she wanted for herself. She had no interest in being a singer, model nor an actress. She didn't want to let me down, or hurt my feelings, so she continued doing the things I wanted her to do.

She wanted to be a computer engineer. I felt so stupid, because I had invested a lot of time and money in my child. I felt my parents should have invested in me. I was talented, outgoing, motivated and smart. But my parent didn't see it. They were too busy making up for lost time that they missed out on. It wasn't a generation circle between me and my child, because I was living my childhood dream through my child and my parents were living their lives trying to stay on top, by working hard to keep a roof over our heads.

My daughter was smart enough to let me know she was living my dream and it wasn't something she wanted for herself. I couldn't do anything but respect her wishes. We cancelled my childhood dream and began working on what she wanted to do. I bought her first computer, at the age of eleven and she was a wiz on it. She somehow learn everything she needed to know about computers and was helping her older brothers out, by deleting computer viruses, building web sites and other things that had to do with computers.

She put a hundred percent into what she was doing and she really enjoys working with computers. She didn't have to worry about disappointing me, because she didn't want to be what I wanted her to be. She was living her life for her, doing what she wanted to do and it made us both happy.

It's okay if you missed out on your childhood dreams. If it meant so much to you, and you still have the desire to do it, then go for it. The sky is the limit and I am still reaching. I won't stop reaching until I touch it. You won't know if you don't try. The only thing that can beat a failure is not trying, and I tell that to my children often.

For as long as I can remember, I have lived my life for other people and during the process. I've made some of the people happy. I know you can't please everyone, but I really tried and the harder I tried, the more I began to realize it was impossible. I was trying so hard to make any and everyone else happy, I had forgotten all about me.

So I started asking myself, what did I want to do?

And that's when I decided to live for myself. At first I was confused, because I had lived my life for other people for so long, I didn't know what I wanted to do. I didn't know where to start. I've never had to think for myself, because others were thinking for me. I felt handicapped, it was like a baby trying to take that first step, but not completely sure if he could do it. I knew what I had to do. I just didn't know where to start. I had listened to other people telling me what to do and how to do it for so long.

I was afraid at first. Because I thought, if I was to take that first step out on my own, all the people that were leading me to go a different way, would turn their backs on me, for trying to do what I wanted to do. Because of this feeling I had, I did what others told me to do. They never knew how unhappy I was. I never showed my true feelings to them. I felt like a puppet, letting others pull my string as I stumbled through life.

It took a while, but I finally found the courage to do something on my own. And when I stepped out without permission, it was nothing like I thought it would be.

Some of the people were happy for me and some were disappointed. I told myself that I wasn't responsible for the ones that weren't happy for me and I continued on, doing the things I wanted to do. I'd hope that the others would someday forget about what I did to them and think about what I was doing for me. After all it's my life and I want to live it for me, the way I thought it should be lived and not the way others thought I should live it.

I took my sister's son in to live with me, because he and his mother couldn't seem to get alone. My sister loved living in the project neighborhood, but she didn't want her kids to be ghetto. She tried to keep her kids at arm's length, away from all the bad kids in the neighborhood, but her kids had a mine of their own.

Her kids didn't see anything bad about the other kids. Some of the kids in the neighbor had to do what was needed to survive for the day.

And that meant stealing, selling drugs and selling themselves to keep a roof over their siblings head. A lot of the parents in the project had low self esteem and used drugs to try and forget about the problems they were having.

My sister seemed to forgot, she was one of those parents that used to escape from the real world, by smoking weed. But when she saw her kids engaging into drugs and stealing, she couldn't handle it. She needed to talk to them, but she didn't know where to start. So she took the easy way out by sending him to me. I wasn't sure if she sent my nephew to me or if he came on his own. But I knew he needed me and I wasn't about to turn my back on him like his mother did.

I had taken on the responsibility that wasn't my concern. It was my sister decision to continue living in the project, even though there was a possibility of her children wanting to be like the crowd. When children are surrounded around lots of negativity, seeing other kids do the unthinkable and getting away with it. Pretty soon, they are going to try getting away with doing the same thing.

I thought my nephew was kicked out of his mother's house, because of smoking marijuana, but I found out later, he was stealing to take care of his marijuana habit. I had no idea how bad his addiction was, until he began stealing from me. Things were coming up missing and I didn't want to kick him out on the streets, because his mother had already done that. I felt sorry for him, but I had kids of my own and I didn't want them to grasp on to the things my nephew was doing. I no longer wanted to deal with his bad behavior.

How could I put him out of my home without upsetting my sister?

Would it be wrong to ask him to leave?

I was so wrapped up in how my sister would feel about me, than how I was feeling about asking her son to leave my home. I was living my life for them and neither one of them cared about me or my children.

When you try to live your life for others, it only makes things confusing for yourself. You began to think about the person you are living for. Not for what you want out of life. But if you have always been confused and unsure of what you wanted out of life, than it's okay to take someone else's opinion. A lot of people see others succeed in life and want to be like that person. But they have no idea, how to get where that person is. They don't know if that person had any trials and tribulations getting to the point where that person is in.

Not all things are easy to accomplish. You sometimes have to go through something to be something and if you are not willing to go through the fire. There's no point of trying accomplishing what you see in someone else.

I was once married to a man that I knew I shouldn't have married. But I was trying to live my life in someone else's eyes. I stayed with my second husband nearly ten years, pretending to be happy. Knowing I was miserable. In the public's eyes, people saw us as a happy loving couple. But things were different behind closed doors. I finally got up enough nerves to get out of the marriage. I was not only hurting myself, but I was hurting everyone else in the household. I thought being with my husband and pretending to be happy would make a happy home for my children. But my children could see straight through me. They knew my house wasn't a home. I was only fooling myself. When I finally told my husband I wanted a divorce, he was so confused. He thought I was happy. Hell, he thought we were happy.

He tried so hard to figure out if he had done anything wrong. But he couldn't think of anything.

So, why did I want out of the marriage?

Who was in fault?

I confessed and told him that I had made a mistake marrying him. I tried to make it work, but I could no longer go on living a lie. The worst thing about our marriage was our son. He was nine years old and I knew it would do some kind of damage to him, because he loved us both and I didn't want him to have to choose which parent he wanted to live with.

I chose to let my ex-husband take care of our son, because I knew he would do a better job raising him to be the perfect man for a woman, because he was the perfect husband to me. I just couldn't seem to let myself fall in love with him. And the more I tried the worse it got. He never judged me, but he knew he had to let me go to keep the peace. I learned a lot from that mistake and from then on, I chose to live my life for me and no one else. Therefore if I make a mistake, the mistake is mine and I have no one to blame but myself.

Sometimes, we as parents sacrifice a lot for our kids and that's a good thing. It's different when a parent decides to live for their children, by putting their needs first and put themselves last. That's an unselfish decision, depending how the child is living.

Some parents put themselves in debt trying to be their child's best friend and parent both. But what the parent fails to realize, is they are suppose to be a parent first, then a best friend. Some parents don't need to be a friend to their kids at all, because they are afraid of making the child upset. So they give in to their child's every need, even if it puts them into debt. If a child starts out earning their money, by doing different little chores around the house at a young age, they will appreciate their money and become a responsible adult, if the parent teaches them how to manage their money. Living for your kids, doesn't mean you have to give up living for yourself. It just means you have other responsibilities to live for. So don't get it twisted, you can still live for yourself, you just have to determine what's more important.

It took my niece years before she decided to live for herself. She started out at a very young age having children, so she thought her life was ruined. She began to down grade herself, because she had to drop out of school to be a mother for her children. It was hard for her to find someone that wanted to keep three kids and the cost of keeping three kids was expensive.

It was best for her to drop out of school and try to get her GED, so she could be a mother to her children and get an education at the same time. But she wasn't able to study the way she needed to, so she could pass the test. Having three children and having all of them in pampers at the same time was hard.

She felt bad, because she had to depend on the system to live. After being on the waiting list for two years, she finally got a place of her own. It wasn't the best of living, but it was something for her and her kids.

She no longer had to listen to people talk about how young she was with three children. When she got her own place, she and the kids had to sleep on the floor. Until one day someone moved out of their apartment and left a full size bed and an old beat up sofa. It was like Christmas to her. She purchased a cover to throw over the sofa and she wrapped the mattress with plastic wrap, so she wouldn't get germs from the people that left the old furnisher. Someone had given her an old television, but it was in good condition. She set it on some milk crates that she got from behind the grocery store, close to her apartments.

Normally she would feel bad about her living conditions, but this was the first time in a long time that she felt as if she was living her life for herself and not for others.

She was proud of what she had. She might not have been where she wanted to be, but she was happy that she wasn't where she used to be. She always tried to stay positive around her kids. She didn't want them to think they were poor, even though they were living off the government. She wanted her kids to feel good about what they had and not to worry about what they didn't have. She kept a roof over her children heads, they had plenty of food to eat and even though she couldn't afford name brand clothes, she kept her children neat and clean.

People had stop looking at her as the girl that dropped out of school at such a young age and started looking at all the positive ways she was raising her kids. She might not have much book sense, but she had a lot of common sense and street smarts. She realized at a very young age. It's not what you have, but how you carry yourself.

For a long time she didn't know how to carry herself in such a positive manner, because she was trying to live her life for others.

She realized living her life for her and her kids made a big difference in her mannerism. She began to see things in a different way.

People respected how she put her kids first and how she held her head up high when she had to sleep with the windows up, because she couldn't afford to run the air condition. Everything in her apartment was given to her and she kept it clean and neat. It wasn't long before other young mothers were following her footsteps. The elderly people loved her.

She was always respectful towards them and she would take any advice the elderly had to give. If it not had been for the elderly people giving her advice on how to budget and save, she wouldn't be as good as she is today. She went to garage sales, thrift stores and bought the bent can goods in grocery stores for cheaper prices, so she could save money. She owed it all to her friendly elderly neighbors.

The elderly never babysat for my niece, but they kept a good look out for her and her kids. My niece was so grateful for their help. She took time out to listen to them and accept their advice. They were the ones who told her to live her life for herself and not for others and she will be alright.

As the years went by, my niece was able to get off public assistance, she got her GED, went to beauty school, got her beauty licenses, opened her own beauty shop and live in a beautiful three bedroom condo. As for the elderly people that helped her. She goes by the neighborhood once a month. She'd pick them up and take them to her beauty shop for free hair services.

This was her way of saying she appreciated what the elderly did for her when she was down and out.

Chapter 7

The Old Saying Is

The first time I heard my oldest son tell his son the old saying: don't do as I do. Do as I say do. I paused for a minute, because I got the saying from my stepmother. It was her favorite phase to say to all the kids in the neighborhood. So I guess it's a trend that follows people throughout generations. We seem to think our children aren't listening to us when we say certain things, until we hear our phrases coming from them.

I used to think I was speaking for the hell of it. My son sometimes made me think, the words that I was speaking to him, went into one ear and out the other. I guess that's where we as parents decided to say our children had selective hearing.

When we think they're not listening to what we are saying, but in reality they really are listening.

When I used to hear the elderly people say things like, keep your enemies close, but keep your friends closer. I really didn't understand what they were saying or why they would say it. But now it's all clear to me. I know that if you have friends, you would share some serious information with them. But if that friend becomes your enemy, everything you ever told, is now public information. They now know everything they need to know to destroy you.

No one really thinks about the things they are telling their best friends, because at the time, they think they're going to be best friends forever. Some girls have boys as best friends and they share their secrets with him.

Depending on how long they've been friends, a lot of information has been told between the two of them. Depending on the relationship and how much information they have on one another. At any given time, one of them can cause a lot of damage to the other's reputation.

There have been times when girls are so in love with their boyfriends, they would do just about anything to please him. They have taken naked pictures and sent the pictures to their boyfriend's cell phone. They have had sex in public places and they have done some sexual favors for their boyfriend as well. But when the relationship was over, the boyfriend wanted to get even with the girl for breaking up with him. The pictures that she sent to him, now becomes a posted website page. All the girl's personal business has spread all over the school and the ex-boyfriends is getting all kinds of creditability from his male friends, while the girl is now classified as a hoer that would do anything to please a boyfriend.

Normally it's a good thing for a girl to want to please her boyfriend, but when they start sending nude pictures to cell phones, being a good girlfriend, becomes a tramp. And the old saying is: (What you do in the dark, will come to the light.)

People do so many things in life and think that they will never get caught. And they probably wouldn't get caught, if they kept their mouth shut. Then you have the young kids that have to have a partner to share his or her dark secret, because he or she is too afraid to do the unthinkable alone. But when they get caught, the other partner in crime decides to tell it all. He or she doesn't leave anything out. They tell everything, thinking it would make things better on their part. But when you do something illegal with another person, you both get the same charges. So therefore, if you don't want the things you did in the dark to come to the light, do it alone, but I prefer for you not do it at all. Because I have a friend that told me, if we were ever to do something illegal and got caught, she will be singing like a bird. She said she's going to tell everything. So that let me know, not to involve her into anything that I don't want to come to the light.

I really consider her as being a good friend, because she told me up front, how she will handle herself if we were to get caught doing something illegal. Friends come a dime a dozen and when you find one, you better hold on to them. I can count on one hand, how many friends I have. And they are always there for me. We don't have to talk or see each other every day, but when I need them, they will be there for me. There are no questions asked, no finger pointing, and no money required. Just downright friendship, for when I'm in need.

I can't stand for someone to lie to me and think that it's alright to do so. I tell my kids all the time, just tell me the truth and you might not be in as much trouble, as you would if you lie to me. Because what you do in the dark will come to the light. It may not be today, and it may not be tomorrow. But it will come to the light.

That reminds me when my mother was living. She used to tell me, never date a person that would put his hands on you. She would say if he hit you once, he will hit you again. It may not be the next day and it might not be the next month or year, but he will do it again. Then she would say if I tried to hide it. It would soon come to the light. Because what is done in the dark will soon come to the light.

I used to praise my son for being such a good kid, because I taught him to be a leader and not a follower. But one day, I got a call from one of his teachers, at his high school and she told me that my son and some other boys had gotten into some trouble and had to be expelled from school for a week. She said that she had sent home two notices by my son, but I didn't received the notices, and since I didn't respond to the notices, she decided to call, to make sure my son gave me the papers to read. She asked if we could meet, so we could talk about my son's misbehaving.

When I made it up to the school, my son wasn't expecting me. So when he saw me, he knew he was in trouble. He had already embarrassed me, so now it was his turn to be embarrassed.

I walked into his classroom nice and calm. I listened to what the teacher had to say, about my sons misbehaving issues. Then I asked my son if he had anything to say to me, and why hadn't he told me about the letters his teacher sent home with him. My son had nothing to say. I could see the shame in his eyes, because he knew he had just let me down. I asked, if he thought he could continue acting out as a class clown and get away with it. I told him that eventually, his wrong doing would come to the light. And this was the reason I told him not to ever lie to me or to keep me in the dark. Because what you do in the dark would sooner or later come to the light. I told him that I had always taught him to be a leader, but I didn't intend for him to lead a circus of clowns. I knew the boys that he was clowning around with and his teacher told me that my son was the leader of the bunch.

My son had always made the honor row in school, but this semester he was going to bring home a C, and that wasn't allowed in my house. I asked the teacher, if she could give him more than enough extra credit work, to make up for the foolishness he accrued. I wanted him to have more than enough work to keep his head in his books for weeks. He wasn't allowed to go anywhere until he completed all the extra work that was assigned to him. His punishment was so hard, he apologized to the teacher and I never had any more problems with him, while he lived in my home.

When he moved out to live on TSU college campus, he thought he was his own man and he didn't care what he did in the dark. Because he was on his own and he thought he was the man. So I let him make his mistakes in life, so he could learn from them. Because what you do in the dark will come to the light.

My best friend's mother use to tell her: (You'll catch more bees with honey than with vinegar.) But we would always laugh at her, because it was a known fact. But the old saying was: (You'll catch more flies with honey than with vinegar.)

So why say it?

We knew she was trying to make a point, but we didn't know why. But later on in life when we were older, we caught on to the saying.

My friend had an older sister that was mean and selfish. But my friend and I were always nice and friendly. We kept a smile on our faces and people could never tell if we were in bad moods, because we never wanted to spoil other people day, just because we were having a bad day.

My friend's older sister didn't care who you were or what you were up to. If she was in a bad mood, you might as well join her, because she was sure to bring your spirits down. There were times when I had to put her at arm's length, because I didn't want to jeopardize my friendship with friend. There were times when I had to just walk away. After all, blood is thicker than water and I never wanted to test the waters and loose my best friend over something silly and uncalled for.

There was only one person that could control my friend's sister. And that was her boyfriend of three years. He was up to no good, but he could control my friend's sister, like he was playing a video game. He could push a button and she would change channels as if he had a remote control to a television.

This boy had my friend's sister's mind so far gone, we would threaten to tell him things she had done, that we knew would make him upset with her, and she would be in our every command.

There was nothing she wouldn't do to please this boy. She was like that bee her mother was talking about, and her boyfriend had not only vinegar, but he had salt, pepper, jalapeno peppers and hot sauce. And he would catch her every time. So actually, my friend's mother was wrong about catching bees with honey than vinegar.

When it came to my friend, you had to have honey, because I was as sweet as they come and I didn't deal with anything sour. My best friend was the same way.

People thought we were related. So we began to lie and say we were cousins. Where ever you saw me, you would see her not far behind. We really understood each other and we didn't care when people would say silly things about us being together all the time. We just thought of it as jealousy. I had her back and she had mine.

We were the bees that would sting your ass, if you came at us with vinegar.

We both found guys that we thought we wanted to spend the rest of our lives with. We both became pregnant and we both had boys. Even though we got married and had children, we continued to be in each other's lives. Sometimes it made our husbands jealous, but we didn't care. We were friends for life and we said we would remain that way, no matter what.

As we got older, we sort of slacked up on seeing each other because we needed to put our families first.

Remember the old saying: (Misery loves company?)

How many people in your life, can relate to those words?

There is one particular person that I can relate to, as if it was just yesterday. This person has been at arm's length with me so many times, I can't even begin to count. I've given her so many chances to get herself together, but no matter how many times I try to be there for her. She always find a way to put me back at arm's length with her. She is such a miserable person. I really don't think she likes herself. No matter who tries to keep in touch with her, she has a way about herself that will push anyone away. I don't know if she was doing it on purpose or if she is just sick in the head. I know she loves me and I love her, but I just can't deal with her jealousy. She is jealous of anyone that has something a little better than what she has. Sometimes she will try to get the thing that others have and sometimes she try to destroy what others have, just because she can't get it or she don't know how to get it.

I've seen others try to comfort her, just to be let down. I've seen people try to buy her love and that even failed. But if you are miserable and need some advise. She is most definitely the person to go to.

She can destroy a happy home in one short visit. She can make up a lie so fast, you won't have time to figure out, how she came up with the strategy. She's very good at what she does, and if you don't like misery. It's best to keep her at arm's length at all times. I really think she's sick. I think she hears things that are totally different from what you talk to her about. You could tell her something and she would swear to God, you said something else. And when you confront her about what she told someone else. She would say, the other person was lying on her. So to keep peace out of confusion, people would rather keep her at arm's length, than to deal with all the drama that follows behind her.

I know that don't make it right, but it is what it is, as the old saying goes.

She would call you on the phone and say she is on her way to get you and take you out to eat, or just to take you to visit someone else, and she would never show up.

People have put things on hold, waiting for her to show up and she would be a no show. The only reason people deal with her, is because she is family and we try hard to keep her involved with her relatives. She is a lot of work to deal with, but she is loved by many. She's been able to lie, cheat and steal for so long, and there will be no consequences for her actions. It just comes natural to her to ruin your day, whenever she is around. She has hurt everyone in the family and everyone has given her chance after chance to seek help, because the things she does is not normal.

Any fool can see she needs help, but she refuses to get it. It's useless trying to help someone that doesn't want to be helped. When things don't go her way, she always has a strategy up her sleeve. She usually tries to use the sympathy card. But she has used it one time too many times.

No one believes her anymore. She is like the little boy that cried wolf. There is no one that wants to give her the time of day.

It's always one thing after another with her and the family has gotten tired of it. The people that get alone with her are the other misery mishaps that no one wants to deal with.

When they get together, believe you me. You want to keep them all at arm's length at all times. Because when they are together, something bad is about to happen and you don't want to be nowhere in sight.

Chapter 8

Survival

I was always a go getter. There was nothing too hard for me, once I set my mind to doing something. But as always, there were people that wanted to see me fail. When someone tells me I can't do something, it motivates me to try harder. I'm not sure if I tried harder to prove people wrong, or if I tried harder to prove to myself it can be done. The worst thing a person could do to me is tell me I can't do something.

Something inside of me just snaps and I can't control what happens afterwards. But when I release that monster, all hell can break loose before I finish my accomplishment. I was born to be professional and I don't stop until my profession is completed. My mother used to say I was a big dreamer. But to me, a dreamer is someone that dreams of something huge, that's going to make them famous or at least noticeable after the fact.

Anyone can be a dreamer, but I'm a doer. When I say I'm going to do something, I do it and when I'm finished, it's always professional.

I leave no room for mistakes, because I take my time and plan my success. So when I'm finished, everyone is amazed with my work.

I don't like using the black card, but some people were amazed to find out, I was a young black female accomplishing nice things, in a professional manner.

Even my father was shocked at my work. When he found out I opened a Children's Salon, he wanted to come by, to see if he could help me fix the place up. But when he walked into the door, he couldn't believe his eyes. There was nothing for him to help me fix. I had done it all, and it was the way I predicted in my huge dream, that my mother thought was to big.

I think he was expecting to some old building and the shop looking like what we black people call a whole in the wall.

I'm not sure where I got my talent from, because I don't know all of my history's background. But I'm not afraid to use my talent. Some people have big dreams and that's all it is, a big dream. They are afraid of the what ifs, that came along with the success of the big dream

As soon as an idea hits me, I began to make plan on making it look professional, and how soon can I get started. I don't like to procrastinate, because it delays my plans. I figured, if I think about it too long, I would think my way out of my accomplishment. Sometimes when people continue to think about what they want to do. They think themselves out of doing it, because it takes a lot of work, a lot of time and a lot of patient. But I have in my head: (Why think about it? Just do it.)

I always told my children not to think about it, just do it. Whatever it is, it has to be done anyway.

So why sit on it?

The longer you think about it, the longer it's going it to takes you to finish it. I don't like waiting. I want to get it over with. And if I fail trying, at least I know I did what I was supposed to do. Remember the old saying: (Nothing beats a failure, except not trying.)

I always give myself a short term and a long term goal. That way, I know where I am, in my profession and when I succeed in one term, I know what I have to do next.

My mother would say I start too big, too fast. But what she didn't know was I thought about everything that could go wrong and what I had to do to make it right.

I did research, by looking up, other businesses that were similar to what I was trying to do. Then I would check out the prices of the other businesses, because all people like saving money. Even if it fifty cent. After checking out the competition I wanted to make sure I had something a little better. It didn't take much to give the people something better. It could be something small, like a sticker or a balloon. Because people like free stuff, it seems to make them smile and make their day a little bit brighter.

The key to survival is to have patient. If you're trying to make it to your long term goal, it takes time, nothing happens over night. You have already accomplished your small term goal, because you have opened for business. Opening your business should always be your short term goal, but you don't just want to open a business. You want to succeed in your business, by staying open. This is when the patient come in, because for your first three years in business.

All the money you make is going right back into the business to keep the business flowing. If you can make it through that, you can began thinking about your long term goals.

Maybe your long term goal might be opening up several businesses, or maybe franchising your business. But whatever it is, you have to be ready. Don't try to hurry and open another business if you don't have the money flow from your first business. You want to make sure your first business is doing well enough to help your second business, so you can continue multiplying your success. This is where most people lose their businesses. They are trying to make it big too fast. Everything takes time. Just think of it as having a baby. You have to go through all the steps of getting pregnant. Then there's the nine months of caring the baby. And last but not least, when the baby comes, you have to have the patient of raising the baby. You can't just have a baby and expect for the baby to raise itself. The baby has to crawl before it walks and you have to think about your business the same way.

If you think you've done all that you can do to be successful and things just don't turn out the way that you planned. Don't dwell on it. Just know that you've done your best and it wasn't your time. This is when you start thinking of doing something else. Hold your head up high and continue dreaming big. Believe it or not, people will praise you for trying.

When people see someone stepping out on faith and starting their own business, they are willing to help in any way they can. They are proud of you for taking that step that they were afraid of doing. So they will help you with your dream, because they see something in you that they wish they had. Some people will even ask you, how did you do it?

They want to know, if it was hard or would you do it again?

And when people asked me those questions, I would tell them to just do it, don't think about it. Because when you think about it, you think yourself out of your dream.

I would tell them to surround themselves around positive people. You always want to be around positive people, because they can give you some ideas that you wouldn't have thought of by yourself.

Some people give you ideas and they don't even know that they have given you an idea. But because you are a dreamer, you take into consideration their thoughts and add what they are saying to your dream if you think it would make your dream a reality.

Survival is holding on to something, even when times are hard. And when you make it, it's the best feeling you could ever dream of. for some people, when they think of survival, they think that it's surviving a death threatening situation. But survival can by surviving anything you put your heart and mind into. It can be something as small as finding a job, starting a new position, having a baby, buying a new house or car. Whatever matters the most to you and you complete the challenge. That simply means you have survived. My greatest survival story, was overcoming the fear of failure. Once I opened my very first business. I would come home and have serious anxiety attacks. Because it was a lot of work, trying to keep my business running and holding on to my responsibilities of owning my first home. I thought I had jumped the gun and started my business too soon.

The first three years were rough and bills were due for the business and my home. I couldn't see how I could make it with my business taking off slow. I thought it would be making lots of money by the end of the first year of business. Boy was I wrong. I started biting my nails and pulling out patches of my hair, trying to figure out how I was going to survive without failing. Little did I know, my bills were being paid at both places and I still had a little money left over to purchase the things that was needed to run my business.

The money was there all along. I was just too nervous to see it. But after three years of what I would call struggling. My business picked up and money was flowing just as I predicted it would. It's just, I thought my business would make money much quicker than when it actually started making the money. Things were going so great. I was able to hire employees and pay them a salary. I didn't have to stay at the business as much, and I was able to leave my employees at my place of business, while I went out to advertise for more business. It felt good to be able to leave my place of business with someone else in charge, while I was out advertising for more business. If that wasn't survival, I don't know what is.

Another survival story was raising my first child. I wasn't ready to become a mother. But, when you play grownups, you have to take the responsibility of what grownups do.

So when I found out I was pregnant. I just knew I wasn't ready to give up having fun and becoming a mother. I didn't believe in abortions and my baby daddy wasn't ready to become a father either. This is when I got a reality check, because I began to think about everything a single mother had to do, to survive taking care of a baby.

As time went on, I slowed down my partying. Saved up my money and got ready for the unthinkable. I thought to myself, if I'm going to do this, I have to do it right. So I became a mother figure for my unborn child. That was the first step of my survival kit.

After accomplishing the first step, everything else just fell into part. I didn't have to think about what came next. It just automatically happened as if it was meant to be. When my baby was born, I had no fears. I couldn't believe the love I had for him. I wanted to be the best mother to my child and it all came from within me.

There was no survival kit for me to learn. It was already there inside me. Whatever needed to be done was done without thinking. I didn't worry myself about the things my child would want. I just made sure he had all the things he needed. And as time moved on, so did we. We survived together and if I had to do it all over again. I wouldn't mind it a bit.

In this mean and cruel world we live in. Survival can be just waking up the next day. We have black on black criminal crimes, where black people are killing their own kind, because of jealousy.

Blacks are killing their own to join gangs, to take over neighborhoods. Our black families hate to see someone of their own race get ahead. They are like a barrel filled with crabs. When a crab reaches the top of the barrel and is just about to get out. Another crab grabs it and pulls it back down into the barrel. It's a no win situation.

This is why I keep myself at arm's length at all times.

If you can't trust your own family, who can you trust?

I know it may sound hard when a person have to keep themselves safe, by staying away from family and friends, but that's the only way I know how to live my life.

I've been hurt so many times, by so many people. It's just hard to determine, who's going to stick the knife in my back next. So to stay safe, never turn your back on anyone, especially someone that you think you know well, because they would be the first ones to hurt you and I just can't be hurt again. So arm's length is my golden rule for survival.

Printed in the United States
By Bookmasters